This Book Belongs To

Forever In My Heart

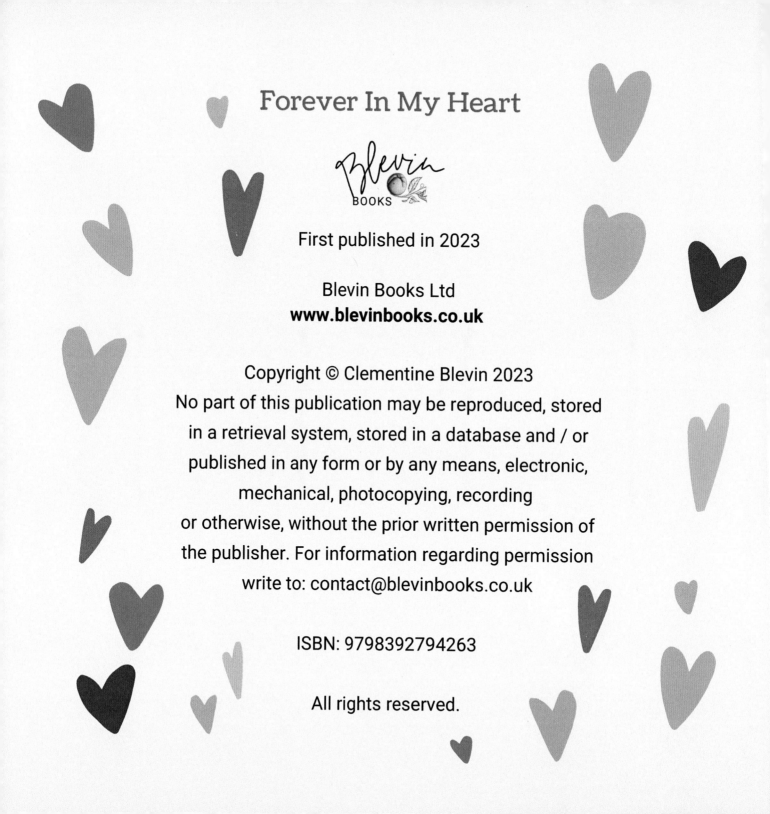

Blevin
BOOKS

First published in 2023

Blevin Books Ltd
www.blevinbooks.co.uk

ISBN: 9798392794263

Forever In My Heart

A Pudding The Cat Story

Clementine Blevin

To Maxie and Mini. We'll see you
over the rainbow bridge.

Here's a little story,
about a fluffy feline gal.

Her very loving owner,
could no longer give her care.

When my own cat Mini,
who was old and quite unwell.

After weeks and weeks of thinking,
of the love I had to give.

To another little ball of fluff,
who might need a place to live.

I visited the shelter,
where cats with no home stay.

They said her name was Pudding;
she had fur as black as coal.

It was as if she saw into my heart, and could somehow understand.

And with that one small gesture, Pudding chose me for her own.

Though Mini always has a place,
tucked in my memory.

So if you had a floof you love,
that had to leave your side.

Remember there will always be, a place for your furry friend.

Inside your heart and memory,
for floofs never really end.

They understand the love you gave,
and would want you to go on.

Giving love to other floofs,
who may have never known.

The joy of cuddles on a lap,
and tickles on the chin.

So don't think you could
never love another ball of fluff.

And when you find another friend,
and begin to feel less sad.

Your old pet will smile, to see you share, the love that they once had.

Forever In My Heart

www.blevinbooks.co.uk

Other Picture Books By Clementine Blevin

Winny The Little Worried Witch

Dream A Little Dream

My Mummy Loves Me

Tilly The Timid Turtle

I do hope that you and your little ones have enjoyed my scribblings.
If this book sparked your imagination or stirred your emotions, I'd greatly appreciate your review!
Feel free to contact me: **clementine@blevinbooks.co.uk**

Clementine

Made in the USA
Las Vegas, NV
03 January 2025